Second Printing, March 1990

Annick Press Ltd.

Annick Press gratefully acknowledges
the assistance of The Canada Council
and The Ontario Arts Council

Canadian Cataloguing in Publication Data

Thompson, Richard, 1951-
  Jenny's neighbours

ISBN 0-920303-70-6 (pbk.) ISBN 0-920303-73-0 (bound)

I. Shoemaker, Kathryn E. II. Title.

PS8589.H65J45 1987   jC813´.54   C86-095070-0
PZ7.T46Je 1987

Distributed in Canada and the USA by:
Firefly Books Ltd.
250 Sparks Avenue
Willowdale, Ontario
M2H 2S4

Printed and bound by D.W. Friesen
Altona, Manitoba, Canada

RICHARD THOMPSON

Jenny's Neighbours

PICTURES

KATHRYN E. SHOEMAKER

ANNICK PRESS

TORONTO

On the morning after the night Sarah slept over, she and Jenny made a beautiful house – a mansion really – under the dining room table.

It took them all morning to move in. They had to bring in a table and some chairs, a stove, a refrigerator and beds for them and cribs for their two babies. They had to move in a whole bunch of toys and books and puzzles, all their dishes and pots and pans and a big box of food.

By the end of the morning they were tired and hungry. Jenny made them a lovely lunch of peanuts and raisins and chocolate chips all mixed together, and grape juice to drink.

As they sat down to eat, Sarah said, "I wonder what our neighbours are like. We should go and say hello right after lunch."

There was a knock at the door.

"I bet that's one of our neighbours now," said Sarah.

"I'm coming!" she called.

A growly voice called back, "Little Pig! Little Pig! Let me come in, or I'll huff and I'll puff and I'll blow your house in."

"Don't you dare blow on our house!" Sarah hollered. She ran to the door and opened it.

"Do I look like a pig to you?" she huffed.

"Well, no, not really," puffed the wolf.

"Then please go away and let us eat our lunch!"

They were just about to start eating again when there was another knock on the door.

"I bet that's a neighbour!" said Jenny, jumping up eagerly.

She opened the door.

A girl stood there, dressed in a flowered frock and a large lace bonnet. She was carrying a shepherd's crook with a large satin bow tied on it. She looked rather upset and she said in a sad voice, "I have lost my sheep, and I don't know where to find them."

"We didn't see any sheep," said Jenny.

The girl started to cry.

"But maybe if you leave them alone they'll come home," said Jenny, "wagging their tails behind them."

"Maybe," sniffled the girl, wiping her nose on her sleeve. "Thank you."

They were just getting ready to eat for a third time when there was yet another knock at the door.

"Who's there?" called Sarah.

A small, shy voice called back, "Excuse me, ma'am. My name is Jack and I was wondering if you would like to buy a cow."

The two girls opened the door. There stood a boy, not much older than themselves, holding a rope that was tied around the neck of a very big brown-and-white cow.

"No, thank you!" said Sarah.

"No, thank you!" said Jenny. "We don't have any hay to feed a cow, and we don't have a barn for her to sleep in."

The boy touched his hat and bowed slightly.

"Thank you just the same," he said. "I will try my luck in the market place. Good day!"

The girls sat back down and started to eat their lunch.

"We have pretty funny neighbours, Jenny," said Sarah.

"They're probably very nice once you get to know them," said Jenny, popping a chocolate chip into her mouth.

At that moment a thundering rumble shook the house. The table wobbled, the windows rattled and juice slopped out of Jenny's cup, making a big purple splotch on the tablecloth. Jenny and Sarah jumped up and ran to the window.

All of a sudden the wolf ran by the window, followed closely by three fat, pink pigs.

"There's a giant coming! There's a giant coming!" the wolf yelled as he dived behind the china cabinet.

The pigs oinked and grunted, grunted and oinked, poked their noses in all the corners and eventually crowded together under the table, spilling Sarah and Jenny's lunch onto the floor.

"A giant is coming?" said Jenny.

"Sounds like sheep," said Sarah.

In came the girl in the frock and the lace bonnet and, hot on her heels, a dozen sheep.

She ran around and around the room yelling, "He's almost here! He's almost here!"

The sheep ran after her, bleating loudly.

Finally, they all crowded behind the rubber tree plant and closed their eyes tight.

The babies were crying, Sarah and Jenny were scared. Neither of them knew what to do. The rumbling was getting louder and closer.

"Maybe we should run away!" said Sarah.

"Yes!" said Jenny.

They grabbed the babies and ran to the door. But just as they were about to run out, the door crashed open and there was Jack.

"Excuse me again, ma'am" he said. "But there is a giant coming and he's almost here!"

And so saying, he ducked behind the dining room curtains and stood very still.

At that moment, a huge dark shadow fell across their house.

A big hairy hand came down and almost ripped the door off its hinges.

A big hairy face filled the doorway, and a deep and rumbly voice said, "Sarah, your mom's here to pick you up. Jenny, come and help Sarah find her dolls and things, please."

When Jenny got back from saying good-bye to Sarah, the dining room table was just a dining room table again.

"What happened to our house!" cried Jenny.

"I had to take it apart, I'm sorry!" said her dad. "The Glovers are coming for lunch and we need the table."

"But what about the wolf and the girl with the sheep and the boy?" asked Jenny.

"They ran out the back door," said her dad.

Jenny went to look, but everyone had disappeared. All she found were four brown beans.

At first she thought she might plant the beans in the garden. But then she thought, "No. I will save them. Whoever dropped them might come back to get them."

If those beans are yours, or if you know who left them, they are still in a jar on a shelf in Jenny's bedroom.

Other Books by Richard Thompson

SKY FULL OF BABIES
FOO
I HAVE TO SEE THIS
GURGLE BUBBLE SPLASH
EFFIE'S BATH
ZOE AND THE MYSTERIOUS X
JESSE ON THE NIGHT TRAIN

Available on cassette:

SKY FULL OF BABIES
(includes Sky Full of Babies, Foo, I Have To See This
Gurgle Bubble Splash, Jesse on the Night Train)

ZOE AND THE MYSTERIOUS X
(includes Zoe and the Mysterious X, Effie's Bath,
Jenny's Neighbours)